LEAPING UP SLIDING AWAY

Kent Thompson

©Kent Thompson, 1986

The author wishes to thank the Canada Council and the Scottish Arts Council for providing him with the opportunity and means to write these stories and others.

Some of these stories were first published in *The Malahat Review* and *Quarry*.

Published by Fiddlehead Poetry Books & Goose Lane Editions Ltd., Fredericton, New Brunswick, Canada, 1986, with the assistance of the Canada Council, the New Brunswick Department of Tourism, Recreation and Heritage, and the University of New Brunswick.

Cover design by Rebecca Leaman

Cover photograph by Robert Wilson
1955 Chevrolet courtesy of Ora MacFarlane

Canadian Cataloguing in Publication Data

Thompson, Kent, 1936 -
　Leaping up sliding away

I. Title.

PS8589.H5L43 1986　　C813'.54　　C86-094347-X
PR9199.3.T564L43 1986

ISBN 0-86492-080-6

Preface

YEARS AGO, walking along a quiet street in Fredericton (most streets in Fredericton are quiet), I heard the anguished voice of a middle-aged man cry out, "he never loved me, he never loved me!" The cry came from a house where there was obviously a family gathering—perhaps after a funeral.

It was an unsettling experience—the voice drew me into the secrets of the house, the past, the anguish of the little boy who was now a man growing old, into a family's private life.

It is various forms of unsettling experience which I have tried to catch in my "postcard stories" which make up the most of this collection. I call them "postcard stories" because many of them were written originally on postcards purchased at various art galleries the year I was living in Scotland as the Canadian Writer-in-Residence in Edinburgh. I bought the postcards because I liked the pictures—not necessarily for their images, but for what they suggested of lives somewhere beyond, beside the pictures.

Having bought the postcards, I wanted to send them to friends—but (o common experience!)—I didn't know what to say. There is not enough space on a postcard to discuss anything. And a postcard is a peculiarly public form of communication—you assume that everyone who handles the postcard will read it—the recipient's spouse or lover, children, certainly the postman.

So I decided to write little stories to surprise the readers. I wanted to make the postman walk from my friend's address in wonder—and you too.

Kent Thompson
Fredericton

THE EXPECTED STORY

Runaway

I THINK OUR daughter is fiddling about with her life. She refuses to give a straight answer to anything. She has chucked the university program in arts management which she was so set on, and has taken a job selling ladies' fashions in Eaton's. Apparently this requires that she wear a great deal of perfume—and be taken to dinner, virtually every night, by a different executive from various corporations. She says this is "looking after my future."

Furthermore, she has upset Sally. Do you know what she wrote to her? She wrote that she felt *marked* by her grandparents' deaths. Couldn't I have kept that secret from her a little longer? She claims that I told the story with some kind of delight, such a *romantic* (her word) story—the shooting and suicide in the bedroom, leaving the lover with the mess. Why didn't he go mad? she asked. How could he return to being a clerk in a hardware store? Was he muscular? she wanted to know. Was he hairy?

You see—she blames me for telling her the story, involving her in my history—and yet she wants more details, details none of us could know. Her imagination is running away with her, you know. I am afraid to think where it might lead her.

Affordable Pleasures

"Sorry I'm late."
"That's all right."
"Just one of those things. Is there any of that cheese?"
"What cheese?"
"That sliced cheese."
"You mean the Kraft Cheese slices that Bobby likes?"
"Yes."
"I don't know. Maybe Bobby ate them all. I *wondered* why we were going through so much of that stuff. He eats it like popcorn or something. Wanders in and takes a slice and wanders out. Now you're doing it too."
"There are worse things."
"That stuff's expensive, you know. I'm trying to get him to eat carrots."
"Yeah. Well—it's one of those things, eh? One of the small things that makes life worth living. The affordable pleasures, eh? Like soft toilet paper."
"Why do you lie all the time? Do you think I don't know where you've been?"
"What are you talking about? Jesus! I just walk in here—look in the fridge—and you start calling me a liar. I don't have to take that, you know. I don't!"

Cool Breezes

There was no one else in the laundromat so she hiked up her skirt and pulled down her underpants and put them in the washing-machine. She giggled. That felt good. Her husband Hobie was having the car seen-to at Canadian Tire and the two kids were with him. She was reading a magazine she found on the window-sill when the young fellow ran in, wild-eyed. He had beautiful red-gold hair. "Hide me!" he cried. She was perplexed; she didn't see anyone following him. She guessed he'd probably robbed a bank. She suggested that he take off his shoes and get in one of the dryers, which he did. "Don't let anyone turn this thing on," he said. She closed the door on him; he looked like an illustrated foetus in there. She took her laundry out of the washing-machine and put it in the dryer next to him. When her husband Hobie came in to say that they'd have to have two new shock-absorbers she wasn't surprised. The car had been canted over all the way from Burnaby. She gave him some money and he left. What she hoped was that the police would come running through and she'd have to decide whether or not she should betray the young fellow. But they didn't and when Hobie came back the young fellow was still safe in the dryer. She had no idea how he'd get out, but his shoes were still there, pointing at his hiding place. But she wanted to keep feeling happy—oh, there'd be a depression later, of course—so she remained bare-assed under her skirt, all the way to Regina.

Corn Flakes

We left Roy behind to look after the store. Do you think that was a mistake? So long as he doesn't drink, everything will be all right, but if he has a drink he'll decide there should be a display of Corn Flakes in the window. If he has a drink, he'll call Maisie, sure as life, and it will begin all over again. I don't want another grandchild. If he has a drink he'll have no more responsibility than water. Is that my fault? How can you discipline a kid with so much charm. "Mother," he said, "I've mended your stockings, you can stop crying now." The mess I've made of my life has cursed him. He's now 43—and where would he be without the store? What will happen if I die? If you see the Corn Flakes in the window, stop in, won't you?

Carleton's Boy

Carleton's boy, now—he's always been crazy about cars and not too crazy about farming—even though it's a very damned good farm, eh? You've seen it—good rich flat land and good barn and sheds, a good big solid stone house—dates back to 1830 and it's been in the family since around 1870. But Carleton's boy, he wants to do nothing but fool around with cars and so what they've done is set up kind of a used-car lot between the house and the barn and there are all these damned vehicular failures lined up side by side with pennants flapping over them and you just drive out to Carleton's farm and the boy's mother comes out of the kitchen drying her hands on a tea-towel and asks you if you're interested in anything in particular, and if you say you are she rings a school-bell they keep on the porch and pretty soon Carleton's boy comes in from the fields, grinning and ready to deal. He'll sell you a Chevie or a Merc or a Japanese Fly-Catcher, he says, and what he'll sell you is good transportation, he'll guarantee that much, and if you want to try out one of the cars he'll gas it up from the tank by the barn (which he shouldn't do, of course, it's illegal), and he wipes off the steering wheel and adjusts the seat for you and tells you to drive it around all day and if he's not here when you get back just tell his mother and she'll ring the bell for him; he's helping his father do some disking. What do you think of this one? OK?

So you drive off and drive into town and you hear the transmission clunking and you know it's no great deal and you take it back to the farm with every intention of telling him it's no good, but his mother welcomes you with some homemade bread and says what a good boy Carleton is, what a good son, doesn't even have a girlfriend, isn't that amazing, good-looking fellow like he is, and you have to admit that that's a real fine automobile, don't you?

You know what's happened? I've got two of Carleton's boy's cars up on blocks in my back yard right now, and I swear I'm not going out there again just to create an automobile graveyard behind my house, but what are you going to do with a boy who's so good to his mother? There aren't many of us so good to our mothers.

White Skin

What I think is she should not come into a restaurant wearing last year's shorts after having a baby, all that white skin showing, she has no sense, and of course the baby cries. She's married to Jody but she told Sheryl she isn't sure he's the father. She'd prefer it was Mikey. So Mikey comes in the restaurant and she jumps up and runs over to him cooing and asks him if he doesn't think the baby's sweet. He says to her to go away and quit telling lies about him or she'll be sorry, and she just tosses her hair and says she don't care, she don't care. She's going to make that fellow leave town is what I think, and I don't think he had anything to do with it.

0—100k

We told Jody he was well-rid of the faithless bitch—in ten years she'd be a fat shrew anyhow. Why in God's name did he want to take her back? Well, he said, there was the kid (might have been his; might well not have been his, too), and the support payments. He couldn't make the support payments and the payments for the red 'n black Mustang Cobra GT 5-litre with the sun-roof too. "Jeez," he said, "She'll go 0—100k in under 9 seconds. That's good, eh?" So he took her back. You can hear him gear down for Neill's Corners all the way up to the Crown Tavern and have a beer ready for him on the table when he walks in grinning.

The Electric Pink Sunsuit

MET SUNSHINE SUSIE UP AT MCDONALD'S HOPPING CAR TO CAR, BOY, TIMES GONE BY! SHE WAS WEARING HER ELECTRIC PINK SUNSUIT HAIR CUT SHORT. SHE'D BEEN IN THE BIN, HAD SPARKS IN HER EYE, HEY! SHE SAID, WANT TO TAKE ME HOME I'M WILD. I REMEMBERED A HUSBAND WITH A KNIFE. GONE SHE SAID TO JAIL OR HELL, DEAD. I TOOK HER HOME SHE WAS WILD BROKE MY COFFEE TABLE BUT SHE WON'T LEAVE, CLINGS TO ME LIKE TROUBLE BREATHING.

Farm For Sale

You know Benny Leeds who delivers propane for Majestic? Well, Leon was off in Woodstock selling the two calves and this Benny character comes around to deliver propane to Leon and Sally's place and Sally said all she offered him was coffee and she was just being polite, it was damned cold out there. But their kid woke up, eh? Only three but he knew the word to say to Daddy when Leon got home. He said "Benny?" smiling. O Lord you wouldn't believe it. Leon tied Sally to the bed and then dragged it behind the tractor all the way to Cave Springs. Then didn't know what to do next and ended up crying which embarrassed all concerned. Sally said O the Disgrace, O the Disgrace. She and the kid have left for Toronto. Leon is selling the farm. It'll go cheap. What do you think?

Automatic vs. Standard

She thinks you are angry with her because she took the job in Kingston. She says she was not even thinking about a job in Kingston but she was talking long-distance on the phone to Leeanne who moved to Kingston two years ago to take a job as an RNA at Kingston General Hospital, and Leeanne said there was a job going in the office, so she called about it from Halifax and got it just like that. It made her feel *zipped*, she says. *Zipped* from Halifax to Kingston. But it was a real opportunity, and it wasn't like she was still living at home, was it? She says Kingston is quiet but nice. She says maybe you expected her to come back all slim and trim and she says she's sorry she didn't, but she admits you didn't say anything about her gaining weight or about boy friends, but that you criticized the car she bought because it was an automatic drive instead of a standard transmission which she says you think is better, but she says she got what her new friends say is a real good deal on that car and why won't you understand about that.

The Expected Story

What do the police know? O, this is a terrible town. The park is like a neglected cemetery, full of hungry birds. The girl has confessed—said she killed him because he betrayed her with a 15-year-old girl. Which girl? She says she can't say, won't say, and after a while you get the idea she doesn't care, that she only tells the story because she thinks we expect it (she's right) and that she probably made it up. What she is being is polite. She thinks that what she has done is beyond our understanding, and I think she's right about that, too. The first policeman on the scene said she was naked beside the guy's body and had smeared herself with his blood. She'd laid the knife on his chest like it was an altar. The policeman said at first he didn't even recognize her because she was to him just a savage, that's all, and it was only after they got her cleaned up at the station and into some clothes that he realized he knew her father and mother. She was a good girl, he said, until she took up with the fellow she killed. You used to see her running up to cars that stopped at the lights by the old railway tracks down there, trying to sell flowers to tourists. We thought she'd gone a little bit wrong, but thought she might come back without too much trouble—just by wearing a dress instead of jeans, for example, he said. He might have been right. In her dress in the police station she looked about 12 years old, ready to start over again. She smiled at me, flirting.

The Doctor's Postcard

Have I the correct address? I hope so. Are you still working on bones? Oh, those hot days in Stewey McLaughlin's class, remember? Remember Linda? These days I know my way through the thoracic cave as well as any man—as well as you know bones and marrow. It was always a delight to watch you work. You seemed so playful. But tissue—blood—what are they? Denise stands in front of her mirror putting on her make-up and I think: I don't know her at all. She goes off to do things with her afternoons. I came home to lunch one day and she said what a surprise it was and gave me tomato soup and a light kiss when she left, but no explanation, no word about where she was going. My heart is broken. Hope you are keeping well. How is Helen?

His Story, Hers, His Wife's, Mine

"Go on, fire me," Andrea said. Do you remember her voice? So quiet and polite and level—nothing insolent about her but her dark eyes. Me? I tried not to hear, pretended I wasn't there. But what could he do? They'd broken the first rule of administration. They spent weekends in Quebec City at company expense, for God's sake! Now Andrea walks in with the company slides, and mixed in with them not a few of herself wearing nothing but a grin. She flings them all over Lawton's office in front of his secretary, Mrs. Bostwick, who is old enough to be his mother. But that's not the story. The story is that the next day Lawton tried to murder Jayne by giving her an overdose of sleeping pills concealed in a fried-egg sandwich. Can you imagine? He'd never fixed her so much as a cup of coffee before. Of course she discovered the attempt. What a mess, what a revolting mess.

Blonde

Marsha said she was leaving me and I asked why and she said she needed more space and no, she wasn't talking about a new apartment. Then she changed her mind and said she'd stay, but she was going to become a California blonde. She did. So last night I'm in the tub and she turns to me naked from the full-length mirror and says, "See?—I'm so blonde you can't see me at all, can you? I'm invisible."

THE 2ND PIANO CONCERTO

Marnie and the Famous

MARNIE SAYS that she is really quite impressed with her new husband's friends. All of them are well-known in their special fields, she says, although not well-known to the general public. It is the kind of reputation she can respect. It is different from fame. Last week, for example, there was a famous eye-surgeon staying in the cottage by the water. He came up to the house to beg a hot-water bottle. Marnie said it was funny—amusing—to see the renowned surgeon standing on the doorstep in his dressing-gown begging a hot-water bottle for his bad back. The hours, she said, that he stood beside the operating table must be incredible. His hands, to her surprise, seemed to be nothing special. His handwriting, she said, was no better than mine, and we know how bad that is. But she is quite content, she says. She thinks she has the situation of the first wife well under control, and that she and Dan can only become happier as time goes by.

The Dead Girl

"We did the best we could," the father said. He would not open the screen door; kept it locked. "She had her own room—she wanted to decorate it herself, but we couldn't allow that. Perhaps we should have," he said. "Then when her sister Sherry wanted to decorate *her* room, we let her—because we thought we probably should have let Barbara decorate *her* room when she asked. That was probably a mistake, too. One but not the other, eh? But what can you do? Whatever we did turned out to be wrong, even though we were trying to do the right thing. When we found out that Barbara was running with a motorcycle gang we begged her to stop and she said she had. She lied to us. There's nothing much you can do, is there, when they lie to you. What she did with them I don't like to think about. Have you been inside the Clubhouse?"

"Yes."

"Well," he said. "I hope she was happy."

He walked away—didn't shut the inner door—just walked away, refusing to resolve for me a matter which he could not settle for himself.

Dead Time

There were always things she wanted to know, she said. She wanted to know where the wind went when it came time to rest, and where did water sleep? She would like herself to find a place where she was not always so restless. Her husband? She did not know who I was talking about. She had a *brother*—was that the man to whom I was referring? She wore a large white hat and she sat across from me at a restaurant-lounge called *The Single Perfect Rose* and she sipped at her gin collins. Would I take her home? she asked. She would be ever so grateful if I took her home. I had no idea, she said, how nice she could be if I took her home. There was no one home at her house except her brother, she said, and his time had run out.

Her Famous Talking Dogs

Her famous talking dogs annoy me. They follow me everywhere, muttering their few phrases in disapproval: "Goodbye," "Nice Day," "Thank You," "Good Morning." She torments me terribly. I am made to stand waiting for hours while she inspects her garden. Afterwards she calls for me, and the dogs are always with us, five of them, underfoot. When she has gone out at last and left me alone I storm through the house in a fury, banging shut doors and cursing the dogs, who eye me implacably.

Theatrics

I received an empty telephone call last night. Do you know the kind? Not even breathing, but silence like a question.

"Hello?" I said. "Hello?"

I admit I had been drinking. It had been a hard day at the theatre—the colourful figures on the dusty stage, the harsh white rehearsal lights, the grunting, the stumbling on lines, the searching for understanding.

Elise is confused again—her own life bashing up against that of the character. She wants to cry out to her mother to pick her up, carry her—they are fleeing across the border. It is bleak November, and there is a sugar-beet field to cross.

But her character in the play is a bawdy wench who tosses her heavy blonde hair and wants to seduce the rustic waiter. Oh, the innocence of it, compared to her life! She is reaching for innocence (she'll find it, she's a good actress), but she cries out to her mother, and her fat little-girl legs are not long enough nor strong enough to get her to the border, although of course they did.

The empty phone-call—who can it have been? Her husband? Is he after me? Will he appear at the door? Will he say: "I have come to kill you." A man will kill for his moment.

How we love theatre, all of us!

"This is what I am!" he proclaims, he has fallen in love with the End—POMP! the shotgun blast, the sound trapped in my living room, an echo which disturbs the dust, a memory of an echo, a memory, nothing at all but the past.

"He stole my wife!" he cries.

My body sprawled running on the floor in the flash of the photograph, no time to say goodbye.

There is no one to hear his end.

Black.

Caught

Ella came for a visit today. She's the one with that wretched little wiener dog. Her husband is in prison for embezzlement—caught just one month before retirement! He got away with it for ten years! I call that getting a pretty good run for your money. They went to Florida one Xmas, stayed in a big hotel with an indoor swimming pool bigger than the parking lot, she said. In Florida! But getting caught like that just before he should have got away is hard. I gave her a cup of coffee and a bran muffin and she crumbled more of the muffin than she ate. Her hands are terrible. After she left I looked around for something that dog might have left. I didn't find anything, but I won't be surprised if I do. I swear I can smell something.

Friends

A door slams downstairs. It's worrisome. What if someone is seeking her out with a question?

"Lottie—what shall I *do*?" A friend might appear with a jar of homemade raspberry jam as a gift for Lottie, and then take the opportunity to denounce an ex-husband, then weep for him, and at last confess to Lottie the delights of a recent lover. It's exasperating. Lottie has neither husband nor lover nor ever has had.

What she must do immediately, she decides, is go shopping: she needs celery—and some white wrapping paper. She'll buy her sister a box of good dark chocolates and tie the box with a broad, bright red ribbon. Lottie says to herself that she is all thumbs this morning and wants to get out of the house before she breaks something.

The Son-In-Law

I think Harry's business is theft. He rises late, has several cups of coffee, reads the paper, and then leaves with the comment, "I'll be back later." And later he returns—flushed (but he has not been drinking), and often with money in his pockets. He then drags our daughter up the stairs and forces her to giggle. When they return they say airily that they have been "having a nap."

What I think is that Harry robs houses in the afternoons. It is all too easy to imagine him in suburban bedrooms in the afternoons, picking through jewellery-boxes, looking under mattresses, fondling nightgowns in closets. Words appear in the paper: FAMILY HEIRLOOMS MISSING, and Harry sits with his feet up by the fire, a great hairy beast, falling into snoring sleep. Who could possibly believe that he writes children's stories under a pseudonym!

Canaries

Inevitably, things went wrong. Jamie was to arrive at 1:15; he did not arrive until 2. He said the waiter absolutely refused to present the bill—and what could be done about that? At 2:15 Martha appeared with her new husband, looking uneasy. Then Angélique entered, informing us that she had been expelled from school! Such a to-do you wouldn't believe. Jamie was for attacking the headmistress with a pair of shears, and Martha said *she* would not shrink from blackmail. Then one of the servants forgot to close the canaries' cage and the house was a crossfire of darting yellow tufts and all of us in pursuit. That was the moment Walter picked to appear. Of course he fled. Such a pity. He looked so good, so easy, lolling about at the races.

Aunt Irene

As children, we were shocked that Grandfather Hébert did not scold Aunt Irene for playing with her food. If we had messed about with our own plates of stew like that, his full fury—which somehow resided in his moustaches—would have fallen on us. But he did not say a word to her. Then Angélique pointed out that Uncle Louis was spooning his stew into his mouth like a toy soldier and I laughed—and then we were in for it. Grandfather threw down his serviette and spanked us both, muttering—oddly, in English—and growling and breathing hard. Our mother clenched her hands in despair.

But the summer had its compensations. We were allowed to play in the steamy laundry while Thérèse did the weekly washing, and afterwards we ran shouting in the orchard. We could see the faint Saint Lawrence from the orchard, and because it stretched away to the sea, we felt like birds—we felt that anything was possible. One afternoon Aunt Irene promised to teach us to waltz next winter, but she didn't. Back in Montreal Mother told us that Uncle Louis was not right for Irene, that she had gone away (we imagined an Army captain), and that she was not to be spoken of again—nor was she.

The 2nd Piano Concerto

Louis says that he has no strength left, that the girl has bewitched him. We all know what that means. Madeline is taking the children to Manitoba, where she hopes they can grow up quietly. But he is composing extremely well. He seems to be able to hang unresolved melodies in the trees at night. He says they suit her, and sneers at us.

Children Together

O look here! This is a terrible misunderstanding! It is only that, I swear it. Do you remember the time you made all the birds fly away? You clapped your hands and ran at them and Miss LeBlanc was furious with you. They were grosbeaks—and she wanted them as neatly arranged on the lawn as flowers; you wanted to see them splashed yellow and black across the sky—and of course you got your way. You usually do. But then, you are usually right. Please forgive me for what I said—I shall have to live with what I did. Montreal is grey and bleak, and Madame Gaby's lingerie shop—o satins and bows!—has closed forever.

The Fellow at the Door

We had to sell the horses. I regret that most of all. But we managed to save most of mother's dowry-silver—thanks to the good advice of our lawyer—and the first editions. We claimed that the books were "personal effects." When did any of us last read *Vanity Fair*? Jeremy, of course, was nowhere to be seen— nor was the woman. On Saturday a strange man came to the door looking for her. You can imagine what relationship he claimed.

Obligations

We are trying to keep things quiet—but failing. Madame McKay is by turns outraged and humiliated—she shrieks at her servants one moment, and the next begs their pardon. She is quite capable of going mad, you know. I had not expected that. Yesterday she pitched her daughter's clothes out into the snow. When the maid protested, Madame McKay said: "What else would you do with the clothes of a . . . woman like that?" At least she shrinks from certain words. Not everyone would. And Millward? Do you know what struck me the most? That his skin is so shiny. Yes. He glistens; his cheeks glisten; his balding head glistens. He has quite painfully acquired a pistol, but holds it like an obligation, not revenge. It's a terrible burden to him. I think he has no anger and is more likely to use it on himself than on the fellow in question.

A Decadent Man

Left to himself, Millward would have pretended that nothing had happened, that Julie was away somewhere—vaguely—on a visit. Julie is quite beautiful; therefore Julie must of course be entertained—so he reasons, although he wishes she had been more discreet. But the truth is that he did not find much satisfaction in her caresses and enjoyed her stories more. That was their private life; he got her to tell him stories—stories of her love affairs. Yes, that was very shameful, but that's what he liked. He and Julie had a good understanding that way. He would wait for her to come home and she would tell him what she had done. Was it true? Who knows? Most of it probably was not. Julie soon learned that he had a passion for detail. In return—to make Julie feel that all was "fair"—he pretended to love affairs with her mother's maids, and invented lurid accounts of his carryings-on—none of which were true. While she was out he slept—and woke with anticipation when she returned. He anticipated a story. Now her wretched mother has pointed out to him that Julie has been carrying-on with his best friend. He'll have to do something. He weeps when he thinks of the obligation. He hopes Julie is far away. He'll go to the border and say he lost their trail there. That will do. It will have to.

The Second Husband

We went to my husband's mother's for the winter. We called it a holiday, or said that the children deserved better schools—what we thought we'd find for them up there I don't know—but the fact is we were poor. My husband's shoe factory had gone bankrupt, and he was shattered. He was never again any help to me. It was that winter that Dorothy began to dance to the shadows of the lamplight, and within a year the singing began. A new husband might save us, I thought, but he didn't.

The End of Summer

We did not notice that he had been here until he left—and the girl who worked the cash in the hotel restaurant, who had been thoughtful, was suddenly resentful and sardonic. She rejected Walter's marriage proposal (of course he proposes to everyone) by telling him he was "boring." The locally famous ruby necklace was suddenly the property of Mrs. McKenzie. You can imagine the looks she gets.

A Swiss chocolate shop has opened downtown, and another which sells French lingerie.

The end of summer has been too hot and sticky for anyone to move—except to do something either silly or dangerous.

EDWARDIAN POSTCARDS

The Viennese

WERNER, HERE since last week, says that he especially enjoys Gunn's painting—light, and all that warmth without sky; the curve of the beach, the sand—caught in the repeated curve of the girl's thigh—but mostly he tells us stories of Maddi and Vienna and cakes. To hear him tell it, they ate all day and danced all night. But of course he admires the flesh and says that our lakes make him think only of blue, blue, blue. He likes to think of the sprawl and twist of that girl on the sand, he says, marking the place like a visit from the gods. Then he speaks longingly of Maddi sitting on the side of the bed, sipping champagne.

Spiel Der Wellen

This is serious business. Betty has disappeared. She was performing in a *tableau vivant* at Madame Essen's—only for old friends, of course—and went rowing on the river with an old man reputed to be a millionaire. Was there a frolic? Can you imagine the sublime Betty surface-diving under a lily-pad? But she has not been seen since, and beyond the shallows that river opens up into the sea. Maddi is gone, too—which is less surprising—she can be replaced easily enough in the theatricals—but unfortunately the horse has disappeared as well.

Maddi's Way

Can you imagine Maddi in a maid's uniform—Maddi with her lazy walk? But she was angry with Friedrich when he left her—'though he left her well enough off, of course. She says she had fallen in love with Friedrich, and took the position in the home of the merchant-banker out of spite. She of course seduced the banker—and has since had a son by him. When I visited her she was serving herself sweet hot tea from a heavy silver samovar, her hair loose and her gown casual. The infant son played on the carpet at her feet, and the banker-lover stood at her elbow, unable to breathe for love.

Bosworth

London. Eva was sent here, you know. Friedrich looked after her in the expected fashion. Remember when she wore gold bracelets on her upper arms and danced? And the perfume she wore—summer darkness, lightning! When she exercised she became glossy—and then she smiled! Poor Bosworth is in for a bad time of it. Do you know the cyclists' club—also the hangout for prizefighters? She's smiling there these days, for crowds. Poor Bosworth—does anyone know his Christian name? He looks like a man who must attend his own funeral daily and finds there are no other mourners. The wealth isn't worth it, you know. I'd rather end my days tending bar at Holloway's than that—and may.

Bonbon

Lily's little grey dog died last week and we buried it out at Simon's cottage, then went to Rosa's for a "Departure Party"—as Rosa insisted we label it. Lily of course wept and carried on until she felt quite empty, she said—then she began to look around for a new lover. "It's always that way," she said. "I want to start a new life with a new lover." Well, wasn't Colette the same? But Alfred, who belonged to the era of the small grey dog, felt hard done by. He left the party and is said to have walked the streets of the city half the night, dragging the dog's leash behind him.

Luck

Charlotte humiliated her daughter in public (yet again)—at *Le Champignon,* in Judge McKay's presence. Charlotte told Marianne to leave off caressing the Judge's neck and for heaven's sake to stop smirking. Furthermore, she said, Marianne should not pretend to passions which she did not have. Mimicry was in bad taste and ridiculous. Marianne then tried to flee, but Charlotte would not give her permission to leave and when Marianne began to weep, Charlotte told her to stop her snivelling, that Marianne was merely demonstrating once again what a child she was.

We can only guess what will become of all this. Charlotte is desperately jealous of her daughter. What do you suppose the girl might do for revenge or spite? And when? And with whom? Suppose the Judge the lucky recipient of a sudden wilfulness. O the terror! Wouldn't his jowls shake!

I am decorating my flat with roses—a terrible extravagance this time of year, but then—a poor man's wealth can be counted only in metaphors.

Thé Anglais

Lily and I had tea yesterday at Bourassa's. We had the almond cakes, as usual. That charming waiter is still there. M. Lieutaud stopped by our table to express his sympathy. When he left, Lily asked me if I knew that he had a wife and child in the country. Yes, and a motor-car, she said. You had to wear something like a shroud to ride in the motor-car. She thought that was ghostly. Was that the word? she laughed. There is still no news from the fellow who promised to sort out Lily's debts. She says she cannot bear the thought of being arrested again, and if it comes to that she'll take up with Feather. Yes, Feather! That is the measure of her desperation.

1905

A wreck of a life—that's what you'd call it, wouldn't you? Two husbands gone, and a third—how lovely and charming he had looked that day at the railway station, reading his newspaper by the colourful kiosk!—turning cold toward her. Last night he had said: "What do *you* want to do—nothing? Well, I want to do *nothing* as well." He returned to his reading. He was tired of her and next week when she turned the half-century mark—oh! Time for a beauty to be in her grave! A professional beauty has no business growing old and chatty. Her children were scattered across the world—one son in Canada, another in Switzerland, a daughter—by a different husband—in the States. They did not get on well. What she required, she thought—the answer to her problems—was a Russian nobleman who could give her jewels. An old lady can survive quite nicely with diamonds, she thought, but a poor old woman must wear unadorned black and try to slip into the night like a third-rate actress wearing a cloak for effect.

Lovely Animals

I was in Zurich last week and saw at last the infamous portrait of Griselda and Joachim at Schlieffen's. It is a fine painting—especially of Griselda, in her last good year. She is wearing the huge purple hat with the feather—and far too much make-up. Her skin is the blue of watered milk. She and Joachim stare out at the viewer with the defiance of apprehended criminals. One does not immediately notice that their hands are busy on one another in a mockery of all that is decent. Joachim is displayed in all his single magnificence; he is wearing only his spectacles. Griselda was arrested at the border the next year, you know. And Joachim became an oculist in Metz. I have a photograph of him buttoned up in suit, shirt, collar, and necktie. So sad. They were such vulgar animals at play.

CHANGING TRAINS AT YORK

The Professor's Mother

FOR YEARS the son who became the professor had teased her about the way she opened a soft-boiled egg: she was utterly expert, he said; the tap was exact, and the slice. Nothing was lost; nothing was smeared. It was the work of a brain-surgeon, he said. This morning she ate her egg and thought about her son's death. It had been sudden, a surprise to everyone—an embolism resulting in an explosion in the brain. Her son's wife had telephoned in a state of numbed shock, conveying a fact which, she said, she could not yet believe. He had been marking papers; the term was nearly over; there were his red comments all over the papers to his left, none on the papers to his right. His mother imagined his bald head fallen on the desk between the marked and unmarked papers. She took a taxi to the tea-room which had recently opened in a fine old house. She wore her fur wrap although the day was not cold and it was not the right note for the time of year or the occasion. She told the waitress she was expecting a friend, which was not true. She ordered a mushroom quiche which she did not eat, and thought that at last she could let her craziness out—release it from the house like a thing which left the screen-door flapping.

Colours

Virgil said that to be born black was to live your entire life in a hole. Wasn't that funny? And death? Oh, death was a white afternoon in the barracks square—smashed against the wall by the firing squad.

When he completed his thesis he discarded his fat American girlfriend and returned home to serve several years as a respected civil-servant—a man who was, however, sometimes mocked for his histrionic manner and his gold fountain-pen. "Now, when I sign this document the project will go forward and water will gush from the earth—Magic!" he laughed. He was fat now.

When the water project was completed, and the new government—which spoke no English—took over, Virgil retired quickly and cultivated tomatoes in his garden like an Englishman. He wore a white tennis hat. He was proud of his tomatoes—the great success of his life, he said. From time to time he tore a ripe tomato from the vine with his huge hands and ate it greedily in the warm sunshine. He felt a bit like a savage, he laughed. But in the afternoons he sat in the shade, waiting.

Unreeling

Helen has left me and moved back to 1930. She is singing in a log-cabin Roadhouse out on old Highway 42. Almost nobody travels out that way anymore. She wears an ivory coloured evening gown and has marcelled her hair. Her lover is the owner who sometimes gives ballroom-dancing exhibitions with her. The patrons are kids who stare in wonder—not, as Helen and her lover believe, at the grace of the old ballroom dances or the sweetness of the lachrymose songs—but at the audacity of the two of them, daring to live outside their allotted time. I sometimes go there and contribute to the decor by sitting at a table wearing a fedora. But I think I am slipping out of her memory, and will disappear as soon as I am forgotten.

Changing Trains at York

She asked me to whistle. Everyone in the compartment laughed. The young Canadian officer who said he was her husband smiled, but I thought he was as frightened of her as I was. She was very beautiful.

"Do you have perfect pitch?" she asked me.

"O no," I said. I attempted a tune: it came out "Yankee Doodle Dandy." Everyone laughed—because there were more than enough Yanks around in those days.

The train approached York, where many would change. She and her young officer got up. They had several suitcases—all of them old, but good, much-used, and I offered to help them. "That would be very kind of you," she said. Her Canadian officer was already busy taking the cases to the end of the corridor, returning for more. "Would you be so kind as to help us get them off the train?" she asked. "There's a stop here of over five minutes—I'm quite sure," she said. So of course I did.

The train stopped, and there was the usual whapping of doors and I helped them with their bags—six of them. I decided she was running away from a husband in Scotland, which turned out to be true. She kept me engaged in pleasantries until she heard the guard's whistle. Then she kissed me passionately. The train was moving. It was dreadful. The kiss continued; she pressed herself against me. The train was gone. She released me, smiling. "Now you'll have to come with us, won't you?" she said.

The young officer looked tired. Clearly enough, he saw his ruin before him.

Playing the Scene for Its Conclusion

Imogen no longer acts on stage, you know, but she retains her excellent understanding for the ends of things. One glance and she knows where she will go, how the last scene (Bodley sent away, head down, dragging his suitcase back to his wife) will be played. But oh, what a story she has! Pulled him out of a train, you know—quite literally—made him help us with our luggage and stood kissing him on the platform at York until the train drew away with his old life. I was then playing the part of a Canadian officer. It was all I could do to persuade her not to murder her husband in Edinburgh. How she hated him! But from that day to this Bodley has lived with us like the servant of our dreams.

Working Both Sides

If I got off the train at this place, right here, right now, at this place I refuse to name, how would I live—considering my clothes, my hat, my accent? I'd have to turn to crime. Could I do that? Last night I killed two men without the least difficulty or remorse, but that was in a dream, and it remains to be seen if I can smash a hand with a baseball bat when it protects the till and I'm hungry.

Leaping Up, Sliding Away

On the page the O'Reilly, who had landed at the plantation only the week before, off the riverboat which had later exploded, killing all, a terrible tragedy, leaned against the doorway of Deborah's bedroom. His insolent eyes took her in. He seemed to know her secrets. In a moment, she thought, he was going to walk in boldly. He was going to take the mirror out of her hand and kiss her, he was going to treat her roughly, bad, horribly.

—Edna looked up from the page, out the window of the train, continuing the other's thoughts. He'd rip her clothes off, lock her naked in her room until her father returned and then there'd be a duel. Well, she'd think about that later.

She pulled the cardigan close around her. The landscape leaped past—yes, leaped. Wherever she looked she was caught unawares. A house flew away. The player in the photograph in that fellow's newspaper headed the ball past the screaming fingers of the goal-keeper.

She couldn't help reading. NO SMOKING. Penalty of £50 maximum. *The Winter of Our Love. Star*bride. Words were a comfort.

The man coming back from the buffet swayed toward her and beer splashed out and hit the floor just by her seat. Bastard! Villain! Kill, Cut Throat, Blood splashed on the floor, soaked into the blue carpet, the body fell thudding down.

"Uh," he said.

She turned her head, ignored him, let the landscape slip smoothly away from his body. When you look behind you, she thought, the landscape does not leap but slides.

The Opportune Moment

When Laura and I got back to our bed-and-breakfast place we found the fellow—very Scottish-looking, savage hair, possibly drunk but calm—walking big as life out of our bedroom! Like idiots we stood back and watched him go down the stairs. I shouted out something like "Hey!" and Mrs. Warren, who ran the place (and whose name I could not then remember) came out of the kitchen and shouted at the fellow—who ran away pell-mell into the park across the street and beyond. We went into our room to find everything a mess but nothing stolen. He'd just sneaked in to have a quick look-round on the off chance we might have left our valuables behind. There is an amazing number of drug addicts here. Laura's suitcase had been dumped upside-down and her clothes thrown to the far corners of the room. She said she'd never be able to wear any of them again. I told her not to be silly, and she said that was typical of me—to ignore her feelings. Things like this happened to her, to us, she said. It told her something about me, she said, which I would never understand.

The Red-Feathered Creation

Hats are back! Aren't they lovely? I have a new blue felt wide-brimmed red-feathered creation out of 1930 and I slink into Paul's office and sit on his desk when he's out. His secretary gives me an evil-eye which says: "You're not feminist enough, sister!"

Well, I don't care! Champagne at last and small-town girl makes good. We went to Raymond's the other night and Raymond addressed me as "Mrs. Byrne," which he knows perfectly well I'm not, and Paul didn't bat an eye. Paul doesn't want to talk anyhow, hates "discussions," as he calls them, prefers kisses. What man doesn't?

But if you see Jerry—don't tell him where I am. I know he'll try to find out. But no.

Don't you think I would have made a good spy?

Coup de Théâtre

The two Montreal policeman would not have come to his room if he had not parked his car with the New Brunswick licence-plates on the wrong side of the street on the wrong day. They were being kind—giving the out-of-towner the chance to move it. Maybe they thought he didn't understand the rules. But when they opened the door to his room and saw the very realistic toy pistol—a relic of his family past—his son's toy gun when his son was a boy—of course they shot him. They feared for their lives. What a mess. But it was clear that he had been waiting for them. The landlady said that she heard his footsteps cross to the window as the police came up the front walk.

Before that? He was a high school history teacher who one day walked out of his classroom and robbed a convenience store with the same toy pistol—and escaped because he looked so "respectable." The girl at the cash register didn't notice him and fainted when he pointed the toy pistol at her, so he made it to Montreal.

Yes, there had been some unpleasantness at the school. A female pupil told her gym teacher that he tried to fondle her. His wife left him three years ago, and he had little contact with his children, who said he was a difficult man. But his son said he believed in justice. "Always put things right," the son said his father said. Her insisted on apologies for bad behaviour.

The landlady said that he could probably read French because he knew that her *Chambre à Louer* meant Room for Rent. But he did not speak French, she said. He was lost in the language, she said. She admitted that she herself spoke more English than she let on. "It is necessary," she said, "to protect oneself."

TONIGHT IN THE BLUE LOUNGE

Metaphors

THE RESTAURANT wasn't crowded. She told Robbie to go off and play a video game while she talked with his father for a moment. She gave him a couple of quarters, which surprised him. And when he had gone she told his father, Gary, that Robbie was only playing Little League baseball to please his father and so why should he be so hard on him?

Gary apologized, said she was right, of course, but then— "Aw, Jesus, look! He's standing there laughing with that Chinese kid at that stupid game and he won't even run after a simple fly ball, just stands out there until it hits the ground, doesn't even *try!*"

Robbie's mother did not speak for a moment and Gary knew there was going to be a price to be paid for his ill-considered outburst and the cost was likely to be high.

She was weighing things up. She said: "I've been thinking that Robbie and I ought to go back to Saint John to visit my mother for a while—she can use some help in the store—and Robbie could do a year in school there."

What could he say? He could only nod and agree—as if the ball had got by him and was rolling away to the fence. He could chase it as hard as he could and it would still be too late. He'd never been a graceful person and most achievements were beyond him. He hated himself and realized that he'd lost yet again.

Ponderosa

Jimmy's father said to come by the church, they should have a talk. Everybody knows what that means. But what his father said was that he had been out to the Ponderosa Restaurant on Saturday and there were all of Jimmy's classmates from Bible College with their wives and children and they were all happy, why wasn't he? He wanted Jimmy to get down on his knees and pray right there and Jimmy wouldn't and his father accused him of betraying his wife Linda and running around with that other woman—were these rumours true or untrue? They were untrue, said Jimmy. So his father said: do you have doubts? And Jimmy said he did, and then agreed to pray with his father. He decided to take the church at Mount Hebron and renounce the other woman—about whom he had lied to his father.

But then Linda came to his father the very next week to complain that Jimmy was cruel to her—he ignored her, and said cutting things to her, mocked her—was that any way to treat a Christian wife? Jimmy's father threw up his hands in despair. Was he expected to deal with everything? Were not his troubles with his own congregation enough?

He went over to see Jimmy with a shotgun in his hand, said it was a only a symbol of God's potential wrath, he had no intention of using it, no, but it went off accidentally. Blew off half of Jimmy's jaw. It was only God's mercy that Jimmy didn't die—and afterwards Jimmy was a man possessed by the spirit of God. He and his father are on the road now with the Tabernacle Tent, bringing God's message as a team. His father tells the story and Jimmy, who can't talk anymore, sings—a melodious mourning sound which brings the sinners from the back rows to the front to be saved. God be praised!

Why Do We So Desire The End of Our False Lives?

We were staying at this pretty good motel in the middle of New Brunswick, where the old railway line crosses the main highway north, and the Clerk of the Enquiry, fully-clothed, was hanging by his hands from a rope stretched over the indoor swimming pool. "What do you think of this, Judge?"

The Judge evaluated him. "I think you're about to ruin your suit," he said.

The Enquiry was to take depositions concerning safety in the logging industry, or the lack of it. There had been a bad accident—three men killed in a nasty way, whipped to pieces by a flailing cable.

I was the newspaper reporter, there on sufferance.

Why had the judge taken this job as chairman of the Enquiry?

Because of Martha. She was 40—a handsome woman, firm, the secretary for the Enquiry, married to an electrician, happily, I suppose, but the Judge was a Judge. I knew him to be honest but cruel, and I thought that before the hearings were over he would have her staying with him through the nights—and afterwards? Was the electrician a man likely to weigh up the cost of the Judge's death? Did the electrician love his wife? How much?

Wilmot Park

Oh, these terrible times!

Yesterday a window-cleaner fell to his death downtown. The wind whipped him away—crying out for help, they said. Everyone in town heard him cry out, it seems. Once we would have said God called him, wouldn't we?—and we would have laughed because God was supposed to be good, and we thought differently.

The city authorities are planning to expropriate Laura's back garden—where we used to play when we were children and were so afraid of her father—with good reason! Oh, those terrible "talks" we had with him. Remember the shadows and the smell of the damp earth in the place we used to hide from him behind the willows? How delicious that felt! But the city has no right! Except that it turns out that the city does—"for the public good." But who decides what that is? Aren't *we* the public?

Winter is coming.

There are only three of us left, you know, from the night George killed himself. I can remember it better than Laura can, which is only natural, I suppose. She says she cannot remember that George cried out that she had betrayed him, but I swear he said that—did you hear that? Perhaps I apply the word "betrayed" because I knew that Laura was meeting Stoddart in the park that afternoon while George was speaking in Moncton, trying to get himself elected.

It was such a lovely day, so soft. From the tennis court I could see her and Stoddart by the bandstand, holding hands.

Then the party after the performance of *Mrs. Duncan's Return*. You were so good in that play, so funny. And then George's operatic gesture—producing the straight-razor he'd "borrowed" from his grandfather. I thought he had just nicked himself, fooling around. I was not prepared for the red stain on his shirt which would not stop growing even after he lay still on the floor and the police were there, telling me and you not to look, don't look. Surely they covered him with a blanket, didn't they? How terrible love is!

Yesterday Laura and I shared a taxi to the Regent Mall. She said she needed winter gloves and there was a Special on at Woolco. Things are so expensive these days that you have to take advantage of the opportunities when they come along.

You know, I sometimes think that we thought we were like an enemy raiding party in the centre of Fredericton. We slipped into town to dance on our parents' graves at midnight. We thought we could explode Fredericton from within by giving a London ball—with white trellises and red and yellow paper flowers and you and me and Laura in too much make-up, willing to risk anything for happiness, we said—but we couldn't. Business goes on.

Left Behind

This morning it was so cold that the exhaust plumes of the cars ahead of me hung in the blue air. I was driving to work. Perhaps the beautiful plumes obscured the view of the truck driver; maybe his brakes froze. Somebody will know. The truck smashed into the side of the small car ahead of me.

I stopped, leapt out.

I was the first one.

I ran to the little car and tried to open the door on the driver's side but it was smashed shut. There was blood on the inside of the windshield. I ran around to the other side and the door was locked.

A guy came up with a jack-handle and smashed the window. He let me reach through and open the door, then reach in to put my hand on her hand.

She was a young woman wearing heavy perfume. There was a fox-fur hat on the seat beside her. I could not believe she was dead, but she was. She was dead.

Then the police were there with flashing lights, and then an ambulance, and the attendants wrestled her floppy body out of the car and she was taken away. She was gone. Downtown her employer was looking at his watch, wondering where she was. I couldn't move. Time just wouldn't start for me. The blood on the inside of the windshield formed the letter P, frozen. I ached to touch the fur hat, but a policeman came up to tell me to move my car and asked me if I was all right, asked me if I had been hurt in the accident. No, I said, no—but could he tell me the name of the girl? He shouldn't have, but he did, and time started to move again. A wrecker arrived as I was leaving, and in my rear-view mirror I could see a fellow attach a chain to the front bumper of Elaine's little car. At my office I looked up her number in the phone book—a risky thing, but nobody answered, thank god.

I will go to the funeral and pay my respects. No one can stop me doing that. People will wonder who I am. But why is God so cruel as to take her like that—when she was so full of promise, when she had so much life to give.

What Succeeds In Real Life Is Silence

What succeeded was silence, weariness, nothingness.

Anthony, failed actor, took the hostages because he could see himself on TV holding off the cops with the shotgun thrust through the door, saw himself haggardly negotiating on TV. Because he was an actor (he played once in a TV sitcom about a boy who owned a bear, he was a zoo employee), he couldn't imagine anything beyond the expression he would use in the final close-up.

And how was he to know that the police chief was a movie critic? The police chief waited until the blood dried on the body of 37-year-old *sous-chef* Paul Rosen, and then he telephoned Anthony, let Anthony talk all he wanted to, agreed to nothing—and at last said that, well, Anthony might as well come out now. OK?

The chief chose his words carefully. He gave Anthony an emptiness. The puzzled Anthony came out as if it was the necessary next thing to do.

The police chief was shrewd, too. Anthony was kept cramped in the back seat of a police cruiser for nearly an hour, and when they got to police headquarters, a young policeman walked Anthony in the corridors for a long time before they let him into the brightly lit room to let loose all his words.

Rising Star

Jessie says it's a mixed blessing to get a role in a TV series like *Breakfast Table*. The audience loved her and all, she said—the mail told her she was a *very good wife*, and when women like you, that's something—but you can't imagine how all those letters from Coon Falls and Barf, Newfoundland, make you want to dye your hair green. So she's kind of glad it's ending. And the relationship with Don the cameraman (she flirted with him through the lens and projected such unwifely lust that the director had to tell her to cut it out) didn't work out. They shared an apartment for a while. He got upset about something. What she did was take a hot bath one day and lock the door. She didn't usually lock the door, she said. And she happened to call out to him that she was going to Montreal for an audition the next day. When he tried to come in, he found the door locked. What he liked to do was come in and wash her. She thought he might try to knock the door down—but he wasn't that sort, she said. But do you know what he *did* do? He took up with that lady who did the costumes for *Breakfast Table*. She's *Austrian*, would you believe. Jessie says she can imagine him and the *Austrian* doing it in the wardrobe room, and he's probably wearing that crown they have for commercials and nothing else. The *Austrian* is at least 40. Wasn't that mean of him? But at least he was the kind of guy who could read a signal. You didn't have to spell things out for him like he was some kind of kid.

Vancouver Residences

What should he do?

English Bay lies surrounded by neat bungalows and large comfortable houses and smaller comfortable people. That day it was warm and sunny and the beach was full of tatter-clad bodies. He had the magazine open before him to an ad for ladies' underwear. Kathy glanced over at the photo of the lithe blonde girl stretching to show off the designer underwear and said, "That girl is dead—I know her, or did, before she died. She was killed in an automobile accident with her lover, a married man."

It was all too much. He wanted to marry someone and yet, how could he give himself to this casual woman to whom life was a comic-strip, one incident after another without difference. Where was the explanation? Could you, in fact, empty yourself like a glass of water? Was that death? Was there no home but that?

Maintaining Taste

Do you know why standards of taste must be maintained? Because, if they are not, you will be dumped into an ugly gash in the ground when you die, and lime poured over you, and then lumps of clay. No monument and no peace. Peace is what we are after, of course, and peace is the long stretches of green lawn between the stone markers, the lively green grass. Gerald used to muse that grass grows greener over a grave and said that of course it was only natural—and that he feared death in a gunbattle and his body full of bullets because no grass would grow. "A scabby grave," he said. "Mangy!" He wanted to escape that—and therefore bought only the best—the best suits, the finest jewellry, surrounded himself with unobtrusive refined women who came to his side because of the vast emptiness of their lives. Well, he died by the knife, not bullets, and it was a surgeon's knife at that, and the story I have is that he writhed on the table and screamed even though he was supposed to be "completely under," and blood was splashing everywhere. Deichel said that you'd have thought somebody had cut the head off a chicken and let it run around flapping its wings until it fell dead in a shower of blood. But Deichel came off the farm, so of course he would say things like that. Deichel was the man designated to watch.

The Old Car

She'd told her son about that old car, she'd warned him. He hadn't listened and now the cop was at the door, saying they were going to tow it away because it was blocking traffic, because of the snow, eh? The snow was snarling things up pretty good, the cop said, looking back over his shoulder. It was still falling, but it was filthy in the streets already, churned up black and slushy. The city bus heaved and grunted its way around the car—splattering it with great grey splotches. She hated that car. There was a terrible secret about that car.

What happened was that when she and Wally—she later married Wally, Wally was Lenny's father, gone now—when she and Wally met, he had a car just like that. He said, "Hey—perch on the fender, eh?" It was like she was a model. That was the year of the skirts that hitched-up under the bum, and she looked good and knew it. She could perch up there and look good and not give away a thing. Besides, Wally was a good-looking guy, and after the photograph which he took laughing like hell (she laughed with him), he said, hey, why not go out to the beach and the park for a swim and she said sure.

She had just finished high school and was looking around for a job. She knew Wally from three streets over and from the halls at school. They kind of grew up at the same time; maybe that was it.

She felt easy with him at the beach and they lay dozing on the sand, their bodies so rich in promise that they had only to touch little fingers to feel the thrill of feeling good; they waited for dark for their first kiss, and then hurtled south with the windows open. It was crazy. He explained to her that in Boston he could do really good, hell, he wasn't stupid, and she told him how much she wanted a baby, so bad she couldn't breathe sometimes thinking about it, wanted to hold a baby and feel him (it was a him) suck at her. She hesitated when she said the word *suck* because it seemed dirty and she knew that when you said something dirty to a guy you couldn't turn back even if you wanted to. They stopped at a motel and, as he promised, they were married two weeks later, the day before she began to suspect, rightly, that she was pregnant—but safe. Her father would never question it; her mother would never say anything, whatever she thought. Just made it—and the next two children confirmed her in her own mind that she'd done the right thing; she loved them all; loved Christmas, loved watching the kids tear open their presents—and she teased Wally about getting just a little bit chubby, he'd have to take it easy on the beer, eh?

He said did she want him to start drinking the hard stuff, was that what she wanted, and maybe she wanted him to start wearing a three-piece suit, was that what she wanted, like her god-damned father who sold insurance and what the hell kind of job was that anyway? He was angrier than she had any reason to expect, so she apologized immediately. That was the year the three-piece suit was in fashion.

But she shouldn't have teased him—teasing was always bad because it gave a guy an *excuse*, didn't it—because it was after that that he took up with that little bitch Linda. She knew about it; confronted him with the fact. He shrugged. What the hell did she expect, he said, the way she acted. She asked just what the hell he meant by that, and he said she ought to know, shouldn't she? She said she had no idea what he was talking about and he told her to go fuck herself.

It was so god-damned *unfair*. *He* ran around and then blamed *her*. So when she met Gary at church—he was a kind man, unhappily married, liked country-and-western music the way she did—so when Gary took her to the motel she went because everything else was *worse*. That was why she did it. And if it hadn't been for Gary she would have killed herself—except for the children, of course. Gary got her through a tough time. He couldn't marry her; she knew that; she didn't expect that.

Then the terrible joke. Her son Lenny—her and Wally's oldest kid—bought the car, the exact same car, would you believe. Got it from a fellow across the river for $100, which was more than it was worth. She didn't tell her son, of course, although she recognized the car right away. The mirror Wally had put on the underside of the visor on her side of the car was still there. Jesus, that could make you weep. But Lenny got the damn car home and it died out there at the curb. She told him he couldn't leave it there, but he didn't listen to her, never did. Then the snow—and now the police, the god-damn mess, the police telling her they were going to tow it away.

"Go ahead," she said. "What the fuck do I care?"

"You'll have to pay the tow fee," the cop said.

"It's not my car," she said, "it's my son's." And to hell with him, she thought. I warned him, didn't I?

Tonight In The Blue Lounge:
José Lalo & His Marimba

The mellow tones of the marimba balanced the tinkle of ice-cubes (the management thought), and he (without thinking) agreed; the glass of scotch in his paw (his word) looked good; he felt able; successful. He liked the half-light after the glare all day of the office, nineteen storeys up. It had been a good career; he was having a good time.

She was drinking white wine—but shoved the glass two inches farther away from herself; she didn't like to drink (he didn't notice, he was having a good time), it was something you did because you had to (oh, that *boring* music, she thought), like fondling yourself; the glass was smeared with lipstick—that wasn't good, he would think he was out with a drunk, he could do anything to her. Especially when you'd made as many mistakes as she had, control was essential to survival. Her belly was curling over the waistband of her pantyhose, and if she got him into the hotel room she'd undress in the corner; she'd turn to him and smile and she thought he'd like the display of black lace—but how far could that take you? Not home, certainly.

"I like you," she said. "You're a nice man."

Last Sale

Because we were closing down the shop, we didn't want to have anything left over, so around 4 o'clock Heidi, the owner who was going bankrupt and was understandably bitter, told us to give away the rest of the muffins, to hell with them. She took off her apron and said she'd be back at 5:30 to administer the *coup de grâce*, as she put it. She'd had such hopes, and everything had gone wrong. Her lover had left her as well—well, she should have expected it, he was ten years younger than she, but while she was *the young woman on the way up (young* depends on what you're doing, doesn't it), Timmy was very impressed. There was an article about Heidi in *The Star.* Starts with Nothing, Hopes to Franchise Her Smile.

But when we settled in to the long slog of running the business, Timmy got bored. When we weren't laughing and joking and playing up the customers anymore, he started to wander off. Not that he was an employee or anything. He just used to help out, he said, because it was fun. But he said he wanted to resume his career—which meant that somebody somewhere had offered to let him sing for tips in some little restaurant that featured twenty different kinds of pancakes and called them *crêpes.* How were we different? We sold Muffins. We wouldn't have gone bankrupt if it hadn't been for the rent. We sold *lots* of muffins; they were *very* good. But the last day—Heidi throwing things around the kitchen, swearing, destructive, breaking bowls deliberately, fuck 'em—was a rainy miserable day, a Saturday, and there were fewer customers than usual. "Hell," said Heidi, "it was a summer business, we should have known that." She was just going out the door after telling us to give away everything when Timmy appeared. She hadn't seen him for six weeks. She stared at him and said "Go away."

He said: "I hear you've had bad luck."

She said yes, she had.

He said he'd like to buy a bag of muffins. She started to say he could have them for free, but stopped herself. "Last muffins are expensive," she said. "$20."

"Ah shit," he said. He didn't like her playing games with him. He turned and walked away—a tall young man in jeans and leather jacket. When he was gone Heidi started to weep. "Everything's gone, *everything*," she said.

The Sun On Mount Royal

When she got off the elevator she saw Larry sitting on the floor outside her door—head slumped over. He looked like a suit of clothes which had slipped off its hanger—and she was angry with him. He was such a betrayal of his own promise. He was a senior pilot with an American airline, he had succeeded—and now he seemed willing—no, *anxious*, to throw his career away. Couldn't he understand her feelings? She'd made a bad marriage but made the best of it in the small town, and she didn't leave her husband until the last child was packed off to university. Then, she said, without the demands of maternal duty, while she was still attractive (she was, very), she cut herself free of a man who came home at 3 a.m. to vomit.

She had skills, so she fled to Montreal and took the nice flat with the morning view of the mountain, and tried to live well. She took great satisfaction in drinking thick dark coffee alone in the morning, watching the sun sparkle on snowy Mount Royal.

Then she met Larry in an art gallery on Sherbrooke—he followed her outside to ask her to go with him to another gallery next door, and she agreed—she thought he was ideal: handsome, divorced, neat, lively. But every man has a secret, she discovered. His was poetry. He wrote poetry. He wanted to give up flying. "Don't you see?" he said. "In poetry I can stay in flight forever." He flapped his arms, grinned. She thought he was silly.

But she knew what he meant. She was no fool. But he was a terrible burden to her, and she wondered if she could get into her apartment without waking him—if he was asleep.

But as she approached he raised his head and looked at her with terrible eyes. She was going to have to love him. Was this to be the end of her story?

A Writer

35 years ago she wrote:

"...the brightness of the blade cries out for use—the flash of it, and the ease with which it slips into the body to probe for secrets. The *thump* you hear is the hilt—saying far enough, far enough. Now let the blood out. Your enemy is washed out to sea."

But she walks painfully now. Her house—now—is muffled, full of heavy, over-stuffed furniture and pillows—pillows and velvet drapes, dark green and dark red, pulled closed—and oriental rugs over carpets. She smokes a cigarette constantly and carries one of those little beanbag ashtrays which you can set down anyplace—she is the only one allowed to smoke in her house. She turns on a lamp, but there is scant light, only a glow. She lets the smoke veil her face. "Words are so quiet," she says, "so insidious—they linger." She doesn't bother smiling anymore.

How she enjoyed it, always, telling lies!

The Reader

What child can resist the temptation? Which of you has?

Left alone in the house on a warm Sunday afternoon, I explored my mother's lingerie drawer.

Oh, the alluring garments—light as water, agonizingly cool, light as breezes, thrilling, wicked! How they played against the warmth of my hand! Cool sunlight!

I knew my parents were at odds with one another. Why? Who knows why? He bought a new car. She shouted at him for that. She threw away one of his shotguns. Yes—threw it away—stuck it in the garbage! I remember the two garbage-men noticing the barrel sticking up out of the garbage-can and approaching it warily, one from each side, as if it had to be taken by surprise—and then the argument which broke out immediately over claimant's rights. They almost came to blows. The driver got out of the cab to settle the dispute—he took the gun. All three stared at our house; I stared back at them from my window.

Of course my father was beside himself with fury. What *right* did she have?

She said she would not have guns in the house. She would not support that sort of thing.

I found the letters beneath the unopened packets of pantyhose. They were not well-hidden. I think now she meant for my father to find them—to bring their lives to a crisis, to break matters one way or another. But why didn't she think of me? All children explore.

The letters were typed. They were dated. One had arrived only yesterday. They were signed with an initial. They spoke of the delights of my mother's body and praised her ingenious use of it. My mother! They spoke of her warmth, her liquids, her smells. My Mother!

I put the letters back and could not bear to look again.

My parents are reconciled and continue to hold one another at a distance.

I keep the secret within me and it is like holding my breath; I think my heart shall burst.

O mother, why didn't you think of me!

Secrets Of The City

Harry said: "Today's the day." It was supposed to be a surprise, but our daughter let the cat out of the bag—deliberately, I think—although she apologized quickly and said I should not tell her father. I think she's afraid of her father, and I embarrass her. She is terrified that I will look silly or cheap and it will reflect upon her—as if she hadn't chosen her mother carefully.

"Look for something *good*," she told me. "For heaven's sake, don't try for glamour." I am not supposed to want glamour. The glamour I once had is now seen to have been a *mistake*—since I've had Linda and Eric.

Harry took me to a friend of his who would give us a good deal on the fur coat. The friend opened the store especially for us and served us coffee. It was Sunday. Harry knows all the secrets of the city. "Pick out anything you want," Harry said. "You deserve the best. Don't be cheap. Don't pay any attention to the price tags."

They had changing rooms because they sold other things besides furs. Harry couldn't understand why I wanted to use a changing room. I told him I'd call him when I was ready and he could come see. So I took off all my clothes and put on the sable coat and called him. When he came in, I flashed him. He didn't think that was funny. "For god's sake don't do that!" he said. He looked over his shoulder to see if the owner was hanging about.

I told him not to worry, who'd want to see me now? What I was was a sack for children—and I thought you could look right through me like one of those sacks they put onions in. You get a fur coat so nobody can see the children. "It's a beautiful coat, Harry," I said. "Thank you."

But his feelings were hurt—as if he'd gone to great trouble to give me a surprise party and I wasn't properly grateful. He felt cheated and I knew there would be some kind of penalty I'd have to pay.

Lisa's Mother

Rex, the charming piano player in the Blue Lounge, keeps an illegal pistol in his room—for the choice, he says. But he rarely thinks of it while he is playing "Lady Be Good," and smiling with innuendo at the ladies perched on stools, sipping drinks, around his piano. Tonight, however, he is feeling depressed, and so allows himself to be picked up by the best-looking of the younger women—who turns out to be Lisa's mother. Lisa's mother has a desperate edge to her feelings because she has just lost out on the chance of a better job in Montreal. She allows Rex to take her home, and the next morning, Lisa, 14, comes down to find her mother in her robe with a barefoot man at breakfast. Lisa is a very promising ballet student, and she fears the effect on her career of her mother's silliness. "At least you could have picked up your underpants from the living room," she says. "Did you drink all the milk?"

Contents

THE EXPECTED STORY

7	Runaway
8	Affordable Pleasures
9	Cool Breezes
10	Corn Flakes
11	Carleton's Boy
13	White Skin
14	0-100k
15	The Electric Pink Sunsuit
16	Farm For Sale
17	Automatic vs. Standard
18	The Expected Story
19	The Doctor's Postcard
20	His Story, Hers, His Wife's, Mine
21	Blonde

THE 2ND PIANO CONCERTO

25	Marnie and the Famous
26	The Dead Girl
27	Dead Time
28	Her Famous Talking Dogs
29	Theatrics
30	Caught
31	Friends
32	The Son-In-Law
33	Canaries
34	Aunt Irene
35	The 2nd Piano Concerto

36 Children Together
37 The Fellow at the Door
38 Obligations
39 A Decadent Man
40 The Second Husband
41 The End of Summer

EDWARDIAN POSTCARDS

45 The Viennese
46 Spiel Der Wellen
47 Maddi's Way
48 Bosworth
49 Bonbon
50 Luck
51 Thé Anglais
52 1905
53 Lovely Animals

CHANGING TRAINS AT YORK

57 The Professor's Mother
58 Colours
59 Unreeling
60 Changing Trains at York
61 Playing the Scene for Its Conclusion
62 Working Both Sides
63 Leaping Up, Sliding Away
64 The Opportune Moment
65 The Red-Feathered Creation

66   Coup de Théâtre

TONIGHT IN THE BLUE LOUNGE

69   Metaphors
70   Ponderosa
71   Why Do We So Desire The End of Our False Lives?
72   Wilmot Park
74   Left Behind
76   What Succeeds In Real Life Is Silence
77   Rising Star
78   Vancouver Residences
79   Maintaining Taste
80   The Old Car
83   Tonight In The Blue Lounge José Lalo & His Marimba
84   Last Sale
86   The Sun On Mount Royal
87   A Writer
88   The Reader
90   Secrets Of The City
92   Lisa's Mother